△ **W9-BJA-956**

The Classroom at the End of the Hall

The Classroom
at the End
of the
Hall

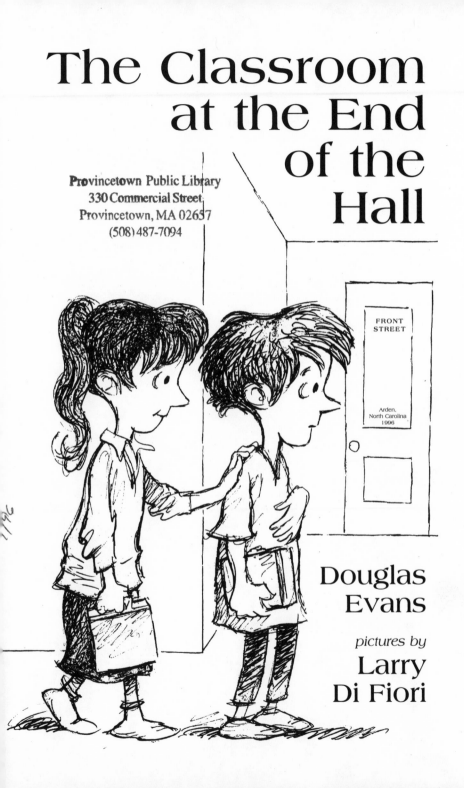

FRONT
STREET

Arden,
North Carolina
1996

Douglas
Evans

pictures by
Larry
Di Fiori

for Faith and Verity Bayley

Evans, Douglas, 1953—
The classroom at the end of the hall / Douglas Evans;
illustrated by Larry Di Fiori
p.   cm.
Summary: Strange things are happening in the classroom at the end of the hall, like a
chalk dust genie that appears while the erasers are being cleaned, and the new art
teacher who resembles a stick figure.
ISBN 1-886910-07-3 (alk. paper)
[1. Schools—Fiction. 2. Supernatural—Fiction. 3. Behavior—Fiction.]
I. Di Fiori, Lawrence, ill. II. Title.
PZ7.E8775C1 1996
[Fic]—dc20   95-48970   CIP AC

CONTENTS

The Classroom
at the End
of the
Hall

Provincetown Public Library
330 Commercial Street
Provincetown, MA 02657
(508) 487-7094

The Classroom at the End of the Hall

"Parents say the classroom is haunted," Mr. Leeks, the custodian at Walter T. Melon Elementary, told us on the first day of school.

He leaned on his mop handle as if it were a crutch. He raised a bushy gray eyebrow and squinted an eye. His whiskers rasped like sandpaper as he stroked his narrow chin.

"And sometimes in the evening when I'm mopping the hallway, I hear sounds myself coming from that room—that room at the end of the hall," he said. "I hear desks banging shut, and chalk squeaking on the blackboard. I hear creaks from the floor and scrapes from the ceiling. Gives me the willies, it does."

Back hunched, the custodian took a few swishes with his mop. He stopped suddenly and stared at us again. The hairs in his nose quivered when he snorted and said, "And let me tell you, youngsters, I've seen things as well in that room—that room at the end of the hall. Take for instance just last night, while I was sweeping the playground. You know how the moon is extra round and bright on the evening before school starts? Well, let me tell you, youngsters, last night moonbeams shone through the classroom windows and fell like a spotlight upon the teacher's desk. And there, as stiff as a flagpole, sat a man—a large, burly man with a bushy black beard. At first I thought he was a wax figure, some store mannequin, but when he raised a finger and pointed to a desk I nearly lost my teeth. Yes sirree, that's all he did, raise a finger and point."

Mr. Leeks swished his mop back and forth, back and forth, as he asked us, "Now tell me, youngsters, can you guess who that man was?"

We shook our heads.

Here the custodian stared over our shoulders. With a shaking, crooked finger, he pointed to a painting hanging above the front door of the school.

Now he spoke in a whisper. "That's Walter T. Melon himself, I'm telling you. The very man I saw in the room at the end of the hall. They say he was a great teacher at one time. They say he was the very best of them. But let me tell you"—and he leaned toward us so that we could smell his sour breath—"they also say that man died some twenty years back."

The custodian wiped his thin lips with the back of his hand. Again he leaned on his mop handle and stared down the hall as if studying our classroom door on the far end.

"I'm telling you, youngsters, and I can't put my finger on it exactly, but something odd, something strange, something peculiar . . ." He stopped and stared right through us. "Something extraordinary goes on in that room at the end of the hall."

Mr. Leeks plunged his mop into the water bucket. "Now the bell is about to ring, youngsters," he said, pushing hard on a lever to squeeze out the mop. "Hope you have yourselves a fine school year."

The Chalk-Dust Genie

Clap! Clap! went the erasers in Roger's hands.
Clap! Clap! Clap! He pounded the felt blocks
together again. *Clap! Clap!* With each wallop, a
large puff of white chalkdust spouted into the
air and drifted across the playground. *Clap!*
Clap! Clap!

Cleaning erasers was the perfect classroom
chore for Roger. What other job gave him a
chance to smash things together? Where else

could he make such a mess and not get in trouble? When else could he be so remarkably noisy without a teacher complaining? For Roger enjoyed nothing more than hitting and making messes and being noisy.

In the classroom, he relished kicking over loaded wastebaskets and grinding pencils in the sharpener for as long and as loudly as possible. It thrilled him to spit in the fish tank, scribble shocking words on his neighbor's desktop with a permanent felt pen, or Super-Glue the lunchboxes in the coat closet together. Nothing felt better than to shout out in class, tell the sickest joke to a first-grader, or do something gross such as writing his name on the blackboard with snot.

In short, Roger was the class Pain-in-the-Neck. No wonder every student in the room at the end of the hall, not to mention the tall teacher, was glad Roger stood outside right now cleaning erasers.

Roger scratched the side of his freckled nose with an eraser, leaving a white blotch on his cheek. Five chalk-dust rectangles already decorated his jeans. He slapped his knee with the eraser and printed one more.

"Now for the final whack," he said, spreading his arms wide. "I might as well go back in the classroom. I mean, math must be over by now." Then swiftly, fiercely, he swung the two erasers together.

Clap! Out billowed a large, powdery chalk cloud. Instead of sailing through the climbing structure and over the swings and slide, however, this white dust hovered in front of the boy like a plump ghost.

Roger blinked twice to make sure he saw what he thought he saw. Yes, smack in the middle of the chalk cloud, gently bobbing up and

down, sat a genie. It had to be a genie. Not only did he wear a golden turban, a large gold ring in his ear, and baggy pajama bottoms, but the first thing he said was, "Your wish is my command, Rog."

A grin stretched across Roger's face. He had read books about genies and knew what they were good for.

"You mean I get three wishes?" he asked. "You mean I can ask for anything I want?"

The genie folded his beefy arms across his bare chest. Raising his smooth chin, he replied in a baritone voice, "You got it, Rog. Care to try one out?"

What better news could a boy like Roger hope for? His brain waves were spinning. Three wishes! Think of the possibilities!

Roger scratched his head with his eraser, streaking his black hair. "Now what could my first wish be?" he said. "I mean, I don't want to waste a good wish, right? I mean, a kid doesn't get a chance like this every day. This wish must be perfect. This wish must do something spectacular . . ."

While he thought, Roger's eyes fell upon the kindergartners, who were out for recess. Instantly his face lit up. Picking on kindergartners was one of his favorite pastimes. He never tired of seeing the surprised looks on the faces of these W. T. Melon newcomers when he did something particularly nasty to them.

Turning toward the genie still bobbing in front of him, Roger said, "Genie, here is my wish. I know just what you can grant me. I wonder what would happen . . . I mean, I don't want anyone to get hurt or anything. But I just wonder what would happen if the playground turned into something slick and slippery. I mean, I wish the playground would turn to ice!"

The genie's nostrils flared as he sucked in a lungful of air. "Are you sure, Rog?" he said gravely.

"Yes, yes, that is my wish and you must grant it," said Roger. "I want to make the playground as slick as you can make it for as long as I say. Won't those little guys be surprised? What will they do? I mean, it will be unbelievable!"

In slow motion, without a word, the genie bobbed inside his white cloud. His inky-black eyes glared down at Roger.

"Well? Well?" said Roger. "Where's the magic? Where's the hocus-pocus? I mean, aren't you supposed to say some magic words or something?"

The genie said nothing. But in the next instant the entire playground turned white,

smooth, and as shiny as a new dime. At once the kindergartners began to slip and slide. Some flapped their arms like penguins to keep from falling. Most were on their fannies in seconds. Jump-ropers crashed to the asphalt, entangled in their ropes, and tag players went skidding into the swings. A girl who was playing hopscotch did the splits, while a chubby boy zipped down the slide so fast that he shot across the baseball diamond clear out to left field.

Roger slapped his thighs with his erasers, plastering his jeans with more white rectangles. "Unbelievable!" he howled. "Did you see that kid go? I mean, did you ever see such a goofy look on a girl's face?

OK, genie, that's enough. Let's not overdo it! Unbelievable! Did you see that little kid spin off the merry-go-round?"

Once the playground returned to asphalt, the genie folded his arms and repeated, "Your wish is my command, Rog."

"Well, now, let me see," said Roger. "I still have two wishes, don't I? I can't waste either one of them. I must wish for just the right thing. I mean, how could I top that last one?"

For at least a minute Roger stood tapping his chin with an eraser. "What if . . . ?" he said. "No, no, that's not good enough." Then he thought some more and said, "I've always wondered what would happen if . . ." But he shook his head and did some more thinking.

Finally Roger tossed the erasers in the air and announced, "Genie, I have it! I know just the thing! I mean, it's perfect! Just wait until you hear it! You see, I want to be head of my class. I want to be in control, call all the shots. I mean, I wish I were the teacher!"

The instant Roger finished this sentence, he found himself sitting behind the teacher's desk in the room at the end of the hall. The green blackboard loomed behind him. Still and silent, his two dozen classmates sat at their desks facing him.

"Well, how about this," said Roger, pivoting back and forth in his swivel chair. "There you go. I'm the teacher and those are my students. I mean, they're just sitting there waiting for my orders."

Roger spun around in his teacher's chair. He opened the desk drawer and blew the teacher's whistle. He rang the teacher's bell and drummed on the desktop with the teacher's ruler.

He cleared his throat importantly and called

out, "Attention, class. Give me your attention, please. All eyes forward now. Sit up straight in your seats."

Here Roger paused to stare severely up and down the five rows of desks. "Is that a voice I hear?" he said. "I want no more chitchat! Emily in the fourth row, stop combing your hair. This is not a beauty parlor. Mary, take that chewing gum out of your mouth and stick it on your nose! Now, class, follow my instructions. Listen and do what I say. I want you to take out your reading books and turn to page thirty."

To Roger's delight the rows of desktops opened in unison. When a reading text lay in front of each student, he commanded, "Now, class, I want you to read pages thirty to thirty-nine. Got that? Then read pages forty to forty-nine. Next, let me see, read fifty to fifty-nine and sixty to sixty-nine. And why not throw in page seventy just for fun."

Roger enjoyed the shocked expressions on the faces of his classmates. "And there will be no talking and no squirming in your seats and no trip to the toilet," he went on. "And, oh, please, please, no questions. Understand? Good. Now enjoy your reading. There will be a big test on it when you have finished. You may begin."

Soon the only sound in the room at the end of the hall was the occasional swish of turning pages. Roger nodded in approval. He leaned back in the teacher's swivel chair and studied the holes in the acoustic-tiled ceiling.

"That should keep this class busy until lunchtime," he said, swinging his feet up on the teacher's desk. "I mean, this teacher business is a breeze. Unbelievable! What a life! I mean, to sit in a classroom all day dishing out orders. How easy can you get?"

In the next moment, however, in the very moment when the room at the end of the hall was most calm and peaceful, when the students were so quiet you could hear the clicking of the clock above the bulletin board, a voice blared from the back of the room.

"What's going on? I mean, what's everyone doing?"

Roger sat bolt upright in his teacher's chair. In the doorway stood a boy holding two erasers. And this boy had the same freckled face, the same chalky jeans, the same dusty black hair—Roger blinked twice—yes, this boy

was a copy of Roger himself.

Whistling a rock-and-roll tune, the boy strolled into the classroom. *Squeak! Squeak!* went his tennis shoes as he shuffled to the front of the classroom. He passed the green blackboard, scraping his fingernails along its entire length. The erasers ended up on the floor.

"Quiet, Creepo!" someone called from the second row.

"Shh! Shh! Shh!" hissed several others.

Leaning forward, Roger followed the boy's progress from the blackboard to a desk in the third row.

"Hold on! Hold the phone! Hold your horses! I mean, hold everything!" he muttered in one breath. "That kid is heading toward my desk."

And that is precisely where the boy sat down. At once he threw open the lid. Crack! Down it came.

"Shh! Shh! Shh! Shh!" circled the room again.

The boy grinned. Without bothering to raise his hand, he called out, "Unbelievable! Hey, teacher! Teacher! I lost my reading book! I have nothing to read! I mean, what am I supposed to do?"

For the first time in his life, Roger, now Roger the teacher, was speechless. Deep down in his gut he knew what would happen next. His eyes fell upon Rosalie, who sat in front of the loud-mouthed boy. Rosalie had a long brown ponytail that hung far down her back. Roger knew this ponytail well, and it came as no surprise to him when Rosalie wheeled in her seat and shook a fist at the boy. She growled, "You put glue on my hair one more time, Creepo, and I'll flatten you."

The boy merely grinned again—a wide, toothy grin that Roger also knew well.

Roger slumped in his teacher's chair and blew out his cheeks. "Someone must do something about that kid," he said. "I mean, what happened to the peace in the room? What happened to the quiet? I mean, how is anyone supposed to get any reading done with that kid disrupting everything?"

Here is what the boy sitting at Roger's desk did next: First he leaped out of his seat. On the way to the back of the room, he snapped Kenneth's reading book shut, knocked on Emily's desktop, and kicked over the wastebasket. At the drinking fountain he took a long, slurpy drink, then burped. Returning to his desk, he made the computer go beep, beep, beep, bumped Howard's chair, snapped Kenneth's book shut a second time, then burped again.

By now no one was reading. The entire class was staring at Roger the teacher, with scowls on their faces.

Roger's shoulders rose to his ears. "So why look at me?" he said. "What do you want me to do?"

But, of course, in his long experience with teachers, Roger knew what the class expected of him. It was his job to stop that Pain-in-the-Neck.

Rattled, he slowly rose from his seat. Pointing a finger at the boy who was now drumming on his desktop with two pencils, he snarled, "All right, you! You will stay in from the next recess with your head down on your desk! Got that? Wait a minute. I mean, you

shouldn't be going outside for the rest of the day! I mean, for the rest of the year! Understand? No, I mean . . . YOU WON'T HAVE RECESS FOR THE REST OF YOUR LIFE!"

As soon as Roger had said these words, he knew he had wasted his breath. How many times had his tall teacher said similar things to him? And what would Roger always do when he did? He would give the tall teacher his wide, goofy smile. And now, there sat the boy wearing the same grin.

Roger's skin grew hot and prickly. He dropped into his chair. "It's hopeless," he muttered. "I mean, that one kid has made the entire classroom miserable. Things were great until he showed up."

There was only one thing left for Roger to do. He stepped to the green blackboard, picked the erasers off the floor, and trudged outside to the playground. Once, twice, three times he pounded the black felt blocks together. Each smack produced a billowy cloud of powder.

On the fourth whack the Chalk-Dust Genie reappeared, complete with golden turban, earring, and pajama bottoms. "Your wish is my command, Rog," he said, bobbing up and down inside his cloud.

"Genie, I don't want to be the teacher any longer," said Roger. "I mean, it's murder. I mean, there's a kid in the class who's driving everyone up the walls. He's unbelievable."

The genie folded his muscled arms and raised his smooth chin. "So that is your last wish, eh, Rog?"

"Sure is. I don't want to be in charge anymore. I want to be my good old self again."

Even as Roger spoke, the cloud of chalkdust rose above the playground, drifted across the baseball diamond, and sailed over the right-field fence.

With the two erasers in his hands, Roger marched into the school. At the door he peeked into the room at the end of the hall. Phew! The tall teacher was back, sitting behind his desk. Every student was hunched over a book, reading silently.

Roger entered the classroom. He was on the verge of shouting out, when he checked himself. Instead, he walked to the blackboard and placed the erasers on the chalk tray. Grinning at his classmates, he crept to his desk in the third row and took out his reader.

After that Roger did a remarkable thing. The class was shocked. The tall teacher nearly fell out of his swivel chair. Roger even surprised himself.

He started to read.

The Messy-Desk Pest

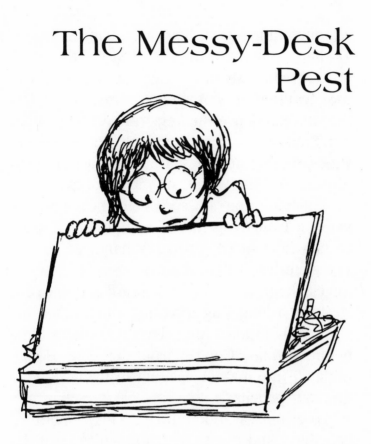

The desk in the fourth row by the bulletin board belonged to Emily. And although Emily was the tidiest girl at W. T. Melon Elementary School, who washed her short blond hair each morning and scrubbed her hands before every meal and polished her teeth each evening, and although Emily wore the cleanest clothes to school—spotless T-shirts, immaculate blue jeans, and the whitest tennis shoes—and although Emily used the neatest handwriting in all her schoolwork and turned in the most orderly math papers, her desk was the messiest desk in the room at the end of the hall.

Not once since the beginning of September had Emily cleaned out her desk. So much junk was collected inside that weeks ago the lid refused to come within six inches of closing.

One morning in early October, the tall teacher leaned against his large metal desk with a mug of coffee in his hand, as he did every morning of every school day. He checked the clock above the bulletin board and yawned. He took a long slug of coffee and studied his class. He checked the clock one more time before saying, "Good morning, people. Happy Friday. Time for our spelling test. Please take out your pencils."

Low noises—one-third groans, one-third grumbles, and one-third gripes—rose from the class.

Emily heaved a long sigh. Whenever she sighed she had a habit of blowing upward with her lower lip in a way that steamed up the round lenses of her eyeglasses. As her glasses cleared, she lifted the lid of her messy desk. Somewhere in that incredible clutter was a sharp pencil.

"Well, here goes," she said. And with both

hands she plowed through the rubbish—the wads of paper, busted crayons, unfinished math sheets, a brown apple core, an empty milk carton fuzzy with mold, four overdue library books, three dirty socks, her bug collection, one hundred twenty-six pennies, three troll dolls, two bloody Band-aids, two hard Twinkies, a brown glob that used to be a Hershey bar, a tennis ball, a golf ball, a moth ball, five mittens, the head of a Barbie doll, six hairbands, a dozen seashells, a four-foot-long gum-wrapper necklace, fifty-three pieces of gum without wrappers, chicken bones, two rubber rats, a squirt gun, and goodness knows what else.

Beside her glue-covered scissors she found the pencil. But its tip was broken.

Emily rushed to the pencil sharpener. "How odd," she said, turning the crank. "I just sharpened my pencils this morning."

By the time Emily had returned to her desk and numbered her spelling paper from one to twenty, the tall teacher was calling out the first spelling word, "There. There are twenty words on this test. There."

Emily blew some eraser crumbs off her spelling sheet and fixed her glasses more firmly on her nose. "There," she told herself. "Cinch to spell."

But the instant her pencil touched the paper, her desktop popped open an inch and cracked down again.

"Hey!" Emily shouted, and every head in the classroom turned toward her.

At the front of the room the tall teacher looked up from his spelling list. He glared at Emily with his famous stare—one eyebrow raised, one eye slightly squinted. He knew how to look at a student to get his message across without saying a word.

"But my . . . But there . . ." She stopped. The look on her teacher's face suggested that she should let him continue with the test.

"Next word," said the tall teacher. "Their. They sat at their desks without making a sound. Their."

Emily was unable to write. Scuffling and scraping sounds, gnawing and chewing sounds, snapping and ripping sounds rose from inside her desk. She put her ear on her desktop.

"Something is in there," she murmured, scarcely able to breathe. "Something is moving around. Something is eating the things in my desk!" And with both hands she flung the lid open.

Inside the desk, next to a half-eaten tangerine, sat a squat, hairy white creature about the size of a potato.

"Hey!" Emily cried again,

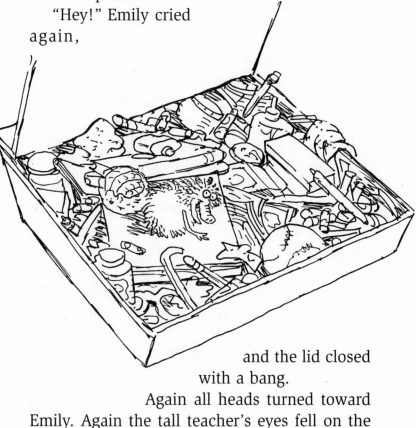

and the lid closed with a bang.

Again all heads turned toward Emily. Again the tall teacher's eyes fell on the desk in the fourth row by the bulletin board. But this time his ears were red, and everyone in the class was familiar with the saying (often repeated as a jump-roping chant of the playground):

When the tall teacher's ears turn red,
Big trouble lies ahead.
When the tall teacher's ears turn white,
Things will be all right.

Emily stared at their teacher's ears. "There's . . . there's something inside my desk," she stuttered.

The tall teacher placed his spelling list on his desk and calmly strolled back to the fourth row. In slow, measured words, he said, "I agree, Emily. I know there is something in your desk. There are many, many things in there. That desk is a mess—a dumpster. It is a disgrace. How many times have I asked you to clean out that desk? How many times has the entire class had to wait while you searched for something in that trash pile? So, Emily, next recess you will remain in this room, cleaning out that desk. Understand?"

Emily nodded. She let out a long sigh, and through foggy glasses she watched the tall teacher return to the front of the room. She thought, "For a teacher who is usually very understanding, why couldn't he be under- standing right now?"

"Third word," the tall teacher called out. "They're. They're trying to take a spelling test. They're."

Although the scratching, tearing, munching, and crackling sounds continued to come from her desk, Emily caused no more interruptions. When the bell rang for recess and the rest of the class stampeded out the door, Emily watched the tall teacher pick up the wastebas- ket.

He walked back to her desk and plopped the metal can at her feet. "Here you go, Emily. Start bulldozing," he said. "By the end of recess I want to see that desk tidy. Not a scrap. Not an item that doesn't belong in there. Understand?" And with that he grabbed his coffee mug off his desk and left the room.

Left alone, Emily gripped her desktop with both hands. She opened it an inch. Scooting her chair far back, she peered through the dark crack.

"All right, you," she whispered. "What's going on in there?"

"Hardy-har-har. Hardy-har," came a reply from behind a lump of clay.

Tense, Emily raised the lid some more. She

leaned forward for a closer look. Her head propped up the desktop. "Who's in here?" she said. "Who's in my desk?"

Some papers rustled. The clay rolled to one side, and the hairy white creature reappeared. Its piggy snout sniffed the air. Its short hamster

ears twitched. When the thing grinned, Emily inspected its full set of ratlike teeth champing down upon the stub of her brown crayon.

Spellbound, Emily watched as the creature climbed onto the math book. With a long, wiry arm it reached up and squeezed her nose.

Emily jerked back her head. "Hey!" she

shouted.

"Hardy-har-har! Hardy-har!" repeated the creature as the desktop slammed shut.

Emily rubbed her nose. She was steamed. She yanked open the desk again and snarled, "Hey, you! Just what are you doing inside my desk?"

The creature grinned again. In a deep, gravelly voice it sang:

> *I am the Messy-Desk Pest.*
> *And I make myself a guest,*
> *In any desk that is messed.*

"Well, Pest," said Emily, "you can't stay in

here. I'll be in big trouble if this desk isn't cleaned out by the end of recess."

"Hardy-har-har. Hardy-har," said the Messy-Desk Pest. "Too bad for you. This is my home now." And it grabbed Emily's glue bottle, stuck it under one long arm, and squeezed.

"Uh-oh," Emily muttered as the glue splurted out. Before she could slam down the desktop, one round lens of her eyeglasses became splattered with white gook.

"Now what?" Emily groaned, wiping off her glasses on her sweatpants.

The recess bell rang again, and soon afterward the class straggled back into the classroom. You can imagine how cross the tall teacher was when he walked up to Emily's desk and found the wastebasket still empty.

Looking straight down at Emily, his ears bright red, he said through his teeth, "Emily, you will not see that playground again until your desk is clean, tidy, spick-and-span, spotless. Understand? That messy desk of yours will not delay our class again."

Emily sighed. She slouched in her chair and waited for the steam to clear from her glasses.

Math period came after recess, and the day did not improve for Emily. Each time she tried to take her math book out of her desk, the Messy-Desk Pest pinched her hand. When she tried to write the answer to 6 x 7, the pest popped up the desktop and her 42 ended up as a scribble.

During the entire hour, the pest's nibbling and gnawing prevented Emily from concentrating on her work, and when she finally managed to open her desk, there lay her favorite monster erasers chewed to crumbs. Even worse, the pest had worn out her new felt pens by scribbling throughout her writing journal.

By lunchtime Emily was about to explode with anger. "I'm going to catch that pest if it's the last thing I do," she declared. And she spent her entire lunch period scribbling on a piece of paper, designing a plan.

After lunch, while the rest of the class was on the playground, Emily sat at her messy desk. She scanned the room for what she needed. On the art table she spied the perfect thing—Popsicle sticks.

She sprang to the table and grabbed a fistful of the wooden sticks, along with a bottle of glue, pipe cleaners, and 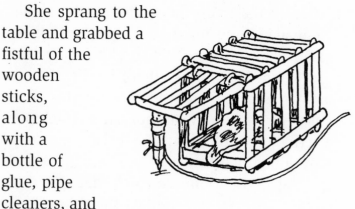 a ball of string. She glued Popsicle stick to Popsicle stick, twisted pipe cleaners, and cut string. When she was through she admired her craft work—a neat little cage with a door that could swing open and shut.

Emily whistled softly as she blew on the cage to harden the glue. For a final touch she stuck on bits of colored paper to give it the perfect messy appearance.

"Now I have a trap," she said to herself. "What I need next is some bait." Here she grabbed a pencil, hustled to the sharpener, and whirled the crank until the point was extra sharp.

Back at her desk, Emily sang out, "Oh, Messy-Desk Pest, I have a present for you. I have decided to let you stay and live in my messy desk."

Thereupon she lifted her desktop and placed the little cage on her math book. With her pencil she propped open the cage door. She tied a piece of string to the pencil and dangled the other end outside her desk. Finally she placed a black banana peel and two blue crayons on the floor of the cage to lure the pest inside. Now her trap was set.

Soon the Messy-Desk Pest peeked out from behind a Styrofoam cup. It eyed the trash inside the little cage. "Hardy-har-har," it snickered. "Hardy-har."

Emily nodded approvingly. "There you are, Pest. Welcome to my desk," she said, and shut the lid just as the class piled back into the room.

Now for the wait. During science period Emily paid little attention to the tall teacher's lesson about magnets. Instead she sat poised at her desk, listening for sounds, one hand gripping the end of the string. At one point, when the room was especially quiet, she heard the deep, muffled voice singing:

> *I am the Messy-Desk Pest,*
> *And I make myself a guest,*
> *In any desk that is messed.*

Soon afterward, Emily felt the string jiggle, and she gave it a yank.

"Gotcha!" she cried.

This, of course, invited more stares from her classmates, but Emily merely leaned back in her chair and smiled with satisfaction.

Not until afternoon recess could Emily check her trap. As soon as the classroom was cleared, she opened her desk. Inside the Popsicle-stick cage sat the frowning Messy-Desk Pest.

Emily lifted the cage and placed it on the floor. "No more hardy-har-hars for you, Pest," she said.

She had to work fast. At once she dug into the pile of mess in her desk. Out came stale doughnuts, rocks, leaky pens, an old sneaker; out came two hairbrushes, three batteries, an unidentifiable green thing, a Girl Scout hat, even a long-lost report card. Most things went straight into the wastebasket.

"My precious mess! My lovely rubbish! My treasured trash!" the Messy-Desk Pest wailed from his little cage. "What are you doing with my glorious garbage?"

After straightening her textbooks into tidy piles, Emily was done. "Now I'll make sure you won't have any place else to go, Pest," she said.

Dashing up and down the rows of desks,

Emily lifted every lid and cleaned out any bit of mess she could find. She even stopped to tidy up the clutter on the tall teacher's desk.

When she was finished she picked up the Popsicle-stick cage and said, "Now, Pest, it is safe to let you free."

"Hardy-hoo-hoo, hardy-hoo," the Messy-Desk Pest cried. "But there is nowhere for me to go. Hardy-hoo! You have cleaned out every desk in the room. Where am I going to live?"

Emily carried the cage over to the window. "Don't fret, Pest," she said. "I'll bet there are plenty of messy desks in other schools. All I know is that from now on I'm going to keep my desk extra clean so you won't ever return here."

As her class came filing back into the room, Emily triumphantly opened the window and dumped the Messy-Desk Pest outside.

Emily sighed. When her eyeglasses cleared she spotted the ugly white creature scuttling across the baseball field. Taking her seat, she said to herself, "I wonder where that pest will end up next."

The New Art Teacher

Charlie hated art. If you mentioned art around Charlie, his stomach would gurgle like a clogged drain. If he even thought about art, Charlie's stomach would go *Spurt! Squeak! Pop! Grrrrrrrrr! Pip! Pip! Grrrrrrrrrrr!*

Nothing Charlie ever created during art period came out the way he wanted it to. His drawings looked like scribbles a kindergartner had done. Every animal he made out of clay looked more like a vegetable. Any project he tried with glue became a smeary mess. Watercolors? Forget it. Charlie's paintings of mountains became brown stains, and his ocean paintings turned to blue blotches.

So now you know why Charlie's stomach erupted every Friday afternoon. Friday afternoon was art period in the room at the end of the hall. And the worst moment of Friday afternoon, the time that sent Charlie sputtering the loudest, was the time when the art teacher hung the completed art projects on the bulletin board.

What could be worse than to have your embarrassing drawing or painting on display for everyone to see? The art teacher always found something kind to say about Charlie's artwork, but how could Charlie help noticing that his pictures ended up hanging at the bottom of the display or behind the door or, worse yet, upside down?

One Friday afternoon Charlie felt lucky. The art teacher was late. Charlie sat at his desk in the front row, both hands on his stomach, his eyes glued to the clock.

"Maybe the art teacher got sick," he said. "Maybe she won't come at all today. Maybe she was fired and we'll never have art again."

After ten minutes of waiting, the class

became squirmy. The noise in the room grew and grew.

"So where is she?" asked Clara, who was the best drawer in the class and was eager for her weekly opportunity to show off.

"We will probably make some sort of turkeys today," said Howard, who remembered Thanksgiving was next week. "Pinecone turkeys, paper-plate turkeys, apple turkeys, or handprint turkeys, what will it be this year?"

And for reasons no one could explain, Roger kept saying, "I hope we do chalk sketches. I mean, I hope we make lots and lots of chalk-dust."

When the classroom door finally opened, Charlie's stomach twisted into a knot. *Spurt! Squeak! Pop! Grrrrrrrr! Pip! Pip! Grrrrrrrrrr!* The sounds rolled out from his lap.

Into the room walked a lady who looked quite different from the one Charlie expected. For one thing, this lady was extremely short, no taller than the shortest kindergartner. For another, she was extraordinarily broad, nearly as wide as two desks pushed side by side.

She wore a long red coat that reached down to a pair of bright yellow boots. On her head was a floppy blue hat that hid her face. A big white daisy bobbled back and forth from the top of the hat as she stepped into the classroom

and waddled like a penguin toward the teacher's desk.

"Maybe she's a sub who hates art as much as I do," Charlie said. "Maybe she's a kind person and will let me do math every Friday. Anything—anything but art."

At the blackboard the lady's gloved hand reached for a piece of chalk. In large block letters she wrote: MISS TRA-LA-LA

Spinning around on the heels of her yellow

boots, she faced the class. From beneath her floppy blue hat came the words Charlie feared: "Good morning, folks. I will be your new art teacher. Your former one has moved to Paris to become a struggling painter. Miss Tra-la-la is my name."

In the front row a low rumble escaped from Charlie's stomach. He quickly dropped his math book onto his lap.

"A new art teacher!" he said to himself. "Now someone else is going to see how lousy I am in art."

As if reading Charlie's thoughts, Miss Tra-la-la stepped forward until her red coat brushed against his desk. "You know, folks, I can tell some of you are not as fond of art as I am," she said, pressing a gloved finger onto Charlie's desktop. "Perhaps today your attitude will change. Now please take out a pencil. Today we shall draw. We shall begin by drawing people."

Spurt! Squeak! Pop! Grrrrrrrrr! Pip! Pip! Grrrrrrrrrr! went Charlie's belly. It sounded like a garbage disposal.

"People!" he groaned to himself. "People are the hardest thing to draw. Maybe we will have an earthquake. Maybe I can hold my breath and try making myself sick. Anything to get out of drawing people."

"Now, folks, some of you might think drawing people is difficult," said Miss Tra-la-la. "But soon you shall see that those thoughts are silly. In fact, I shall be your model. You shall draw me."

What is she talking about? thought Charlie. A person is a person, and drawing a person is torture.

Miss Tra-la-la stood by the teacher's desk and held out her glove-covered arms. "Now I must take off these wraps," she said. "First, my gloves." And when she removed her long white gloves, Charlie got the shock of his life.

"Your arms!" he said aloud. "They're nothing but sticks!"

This was true. Both of the woman's arms were long, wiry, and thin like licorice rope. What is more, at the end of each of these extraordinary limbs, five stick fingers poked out straight.

"Now for my boots," said the art teacher.

Charlie sat in a trance as Miss Tra-la-la pulled off her yellow rubber boots. Sure enough, her legs were just as thin as her arms, and her feet were the shape of pickles.

"Now for my hat," said the new art teacher.

One of her stick arms now reached up to remove the floppy blue hat. Here was a bigger surprise, for the woman's head was as round and flat as a tiddlywink. Her hair was nothing more than two enormous curls draping down the sides. Two black dots served for eyes and a bigger dot for a nose. Stretching from one side of the circle head to the other was long, thin U of a smile that looked so jolly it was impossible to imagine it ever turning upside down.

Last of all, Miss Tra-la-la removed her red coat. Now it was clear what type of person she was.

"You're a stick woman!" said Charlie.

"That is correct, young man," said Miss Tra-la-la. "A stick woman I am."

"Why, I drew stick people when I was in kindergarten!" said Charlie. "I never imagined they really existed."

Naturally, the appearance of a stick woman in front of the flabbergasted class released a flood of questions.

"Are there many stick people like you in the world?" asked Emily.

"Oh, many, many," answered the art teacher. "Stick people come in many different shapes and sizes. Beautiful pictures of us appear in every elementary school and on many refrigerator doors."

"But where do all the stick people live?" asked Rosalie. "I've never seen a real stick person before."

Miss Tra-la-la strutted up and down the aisles of desks, passing out white construction paper. "Why, none of us live in the city," she answered. "We live in the sticks."

As Miss Tra-la-la waddled by, Charlie had a closer look at her stick figure. Perhaps the most remarkable thing about the new art teacher was that her entire body was no thicker than the paper she was passing out. If you looked at her sideways she almost disappeared. You would think that the slightest breeze would have sent her flying up to the lights like a kite. But no, she made her way up and down the rows of desks, sturdy and erect upon those big boat feet of hers.

When everyone had drawing paper, Miss Tra-la-la waved her antenna arms into the air. "OK, folks, start drawing," she called out. "Feel free to use a crayon to color me any color you chose." Then she stepped up onto the teacher's desk, stuck her stick arms and fingers straight out, and stood perfectly still.

At first Charlie did what he usually did when a blank sheet of drawing paper lay front

of him: He stared at it. He twirled his pencil in his fingers and stared at the paper some more. This time, however, something was different. Not only was his stomach quiet, but after studying the stick woman posing on the teacher's desk, he thought, "Maybe I can draw that person. Maybe I will give it a try."

With a firm grip on his pencil, Charlie started to sketch. In the center of his paper he drew a circle for the stick lady's body. Next he tackled her head, adding the two dot eyes, dot nose, U-shaped mouth, and curls of hair.

Charlie sat back in his chair to study his drawing. "Drat," he mumbled. "My head looks more like an egg. It's not the shape of Miss Tra-la-la's head."

Yet when he glanced up at Miss Tra-la-la again, she had changed. Her head was now egg-shaped, precisely the shape Charlie had drawn it.

"Not bad. Not bad at all," he said, admiring his artwork. "Maybe I can do this. Maybe I can draw this person."

With more confidence he added the lady's stick arms and stick legs and stick fingers and big pickle feet.

Now Charlie said to himself, "I wonder what would happen if I drew giant ears on the head."

He did it, and sure enough, the stick lady posing on the teacher's desk now displayed the very jumbo ears Charlie had drawn on his paper.

"Young man," Miss Tra-la-la scolded, "it's grand that you are exploring new ideas in your art. However, it's embarrassing to be standing up here with these elephant ears."

Quickly Charlie erased the offending ears

and sat admiring his finished drawing.

Miss Tra-la-la lowered her arms, wiggled her fingers, and stepped down from the teacher's desk.

"Lovely! Lovely! Lovely!" she said, wandering up and down the rows of desks, admiring each picture.

Back at the teacher's desk, Miss Tra-la-la announced, "OK, folks, for our second picture we shall draw an animal. I'll be back in a jiffy." And she sailed out of the classroom.

Spurt! Squeak! Pop! Grrrrrrrrr! Pip! Pip! Grrrrrrrrrr! Charlie's stomach started to erupt again. "An animal," he grumbled. "Just when I was beginning to get the hang of drawing people, I have to draw an animal. Maybe I can hide in the coat closet. Maybe I can ask to go to the Boys' Room and never come back."

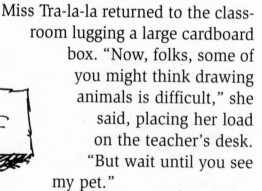

Miss Tra-la-la returned to the classroom lugging a large cardboard box. "Now, folks, some of you might think drawing animals is difficult," she said, placing her load on the teacher's desk. "But wait until you see my pet."

The art teacher opened the box. Out trotted an animal

that Charlie at once recognized as a stick dog. This curious creature had a long, hot-dog-shaped body with four stick legs jutting out from the bottom and a shorter hot-dog head with floppy ears. When it opened its mouth two written words—Arf! Arf!—floated upward and hung in the air.

"That's how cartoon dogs talk," Charlie noted. "Miss Tra-la-la's pet is like a cartoon. It's easy to draw cartoons."

Like its owner, the stick dog was flat. When it wagged its wiry tail, its entire body flapped like a flag. But when it lay on the desk, the dog was impossible to see at all.

Miss Tra-la-la passed out more paper. "OK,

folks, you can start drawing," she said. "Up, doggie," she called to her stick pet. "Now stand perfectly still for these children so that they can draw you."

At once Charlie made a long oval on his paper. He added a shorter oval to one end.

"Maybe drawing this dog is as easy as drawing Miss Tra-la-la," he said to himself. "Maybe I'm not such a bad drawer after all."

At two o'clock Miss Tra-la-la packed her dog back in its box. "OK, folks, that is all the art for this week," she said. "But before I leave I must hang up your masterpieces for exhibition." And she flounced from desk to desk, collecting the drawings.

"Lovely! Lovely! Lovely!" she sang out while pinning each picture up on the bulletin board. "Oh, look at this one! That's me to a T. Look at this and this and that. Lovely! Lovely! Lovely!"

Charlie could have sworn the art teacher's dot eyes opened and shut in a wink when she picked up his two pictures. "Lovely! Lovely! Lovely!" she said, holding the pictures out at stick-arm's length. "Very original! Very avant-garde! These belong in a museum!"

When all the pictures were hung, the art teacher put on her wraps. It took her a full minute. On went the red coat, the yellow boots, and the white gloves. After she covered her head with the floppy blue hat, it was completely impossible to tell that she was a stick woman.

"Next Friday, folks, if you feel comfortable with what you drew today, we shall draw some more things," Miss Tra-la-la said, strutting toward the door. "I shall bring in some photographs of my house and yard out in the sticks. We can practice drawing buildings and trees. Toodle-oo." Then she was gone.

While waiting for the tall teacher to return to the classroom, Charlie admired his drawings pinned up in the middle of the bulletin board.

"Maybe I'm not such a bad artist after all," he said to himself. "Maybe next Friday I'll try a harder drawing."

And as he thought about how his drawing would be, his stomach remained silent.

The Other Witch

Clara drew fierce, dark wrinkles across her forehead. She blackened two front teeth. She plugged a long, crooked nose over her short, pug one, and stuck a clay wart on the end of her chin. Last of all, she pulled a stiff straw-colored wig over her curly brown hair.

Her costume complete, Clara turned toward the mirror in the room at the end of the hall.

"Eh! Eh! Ehhh! What an ugly witch I am, I am," she said in a practiced cackle. "Mirror, mirror, on the wall, who is the ugliest kid of them all? I am! I'm *est*—the ugli*est*, creepi*est*, scari*est* kid in the class. Eh! Eh! Ehhh!" Then she laughed in such a creepy manner that she startled herself.

Clara wiggled her black plastic fingernails at Emily, who stood beside her. "Eh! Eh! Ehhh!" she said. "See how ugly I am, I am."

Emily continued spraying her hair blue. "Brag, brag, brag!" she said. "You always think you are the best in everything, Clara."

"Eh! Eh! Ehhh! That's me. That's me. I'm *est*," said Clara. "I'm the wicked*est*, spooki*est*, ugli*est* kid in the class. Eh! Eh! Ehhh!"

"Brag, brag, brag!" said Emily. "That's all you ever do. Brag, brag, brag!"

Unfortunately, this was true. Clara was a girl who had to be the best at everything she did in school and had to let everyone know about it. Everyone in the class knew her spelling scores were the highest, her book reports the longest, and her handwriting the neatest. When the class made clay pots, Clara's was the largest. If the class sang, Clara sang the loudest. Multiplication flash cards she did the quickest. In dodge ball she threw the hardest. And during lunch in the cafeteria it was Clara who ate the fastest.

So it came as no surprise to anyone when Clara, dressed as a witch, crept around before the Halloween party saying, "Eh! Eh! Ehhh! *Est*! I'm the scari*est*, creepi*est*, ugli*est* kid in the class! No one is uglier than I am. Eh! Eh! Ehhh!"

Lit by a sole jack-o'-lantern, the room at the end of the hall was a scene of fright. Near the coat closet a monster with seven eyeballs pulled on black boots. By the door a vampire with a sinister grin dribbled blood down his chin, while next to him a mummy wrapped herself in toilet paper.

In the center of the classroom the tall teacher stood by a large tub of water. With his

fake black beard and a tall black hat made from cardboard, it was easy to guess that he was dressed as Abe Lincoln this Halloween.

The teacher waved his arms in x's and y's above his head. "All right, people," he called out. "Time to get our Halloween party under way."

One by one the ghouls and goblins circled around the tub of water. Through all the masks and makeup, it was impossible to tell who was who.

Clara was the last to join the circle. While the tall teacher rattled off instructions and party rules, Clara inspected the ring of costumes. She elbowed a one-armed pirate who stood to her right. "Eh! Eh! Ehhh!" she said into the pirate's gold earring. "Don't you think I'm the ugliest kid in the class?"

The pirate ran his unpatched eye around the group. Pointing across the circle with a hook that served for a hand, he said, "Ahoy! Look over there, Matey. Someone else is dressed as a witch. And whoever is wearing that other witch costume has you beat for ugliness. I mean, that's what I call ugly."

Clara shot a look across the circle. How could she have missed this before? Now, as plain as the crooked nose on her face, she spied a second witch, standing directly across the circle from her. And there could be no doubt about it—that other witch's hair was rattier; that other witch's skin was greener; that other witch's nails were longer. In short, that other witch was twice as ugly as Clara.

"Oooooooooooo!" said Clara. "I thought I told everyone that I was going to be a witch this Halloween. So who had the nerve to dress up as the same thing as me?"

Meanwhile, the tall teacher knelt by the tub, dropping apples into it. "OK, people," he said through his fake whiskers. "Time to start bobbing. Who wants a wet face first?"

A forest of hands shot into the air and swayed back and forth like so many trees in a windstorm. The room filled with the grunts, groans, and other amazing sounds students need to make when they are eager for a teacher to call on them.

The tall teacher pointed to a werewolf, who promptly stepped forward and removed his mask. It was Charlie. Everyone howled as Charlie lowered his face into the tub and chased an apple through the water with his gaping mouth.

Clara, however, had little interest in apple bobbing. Her eyes remained fixed on the witch across the way.

"Frances, I bet," she muttered under her

breath. "I'm sure that other witch is Frances. Frances is always trying to do things better than I do them."

But after Charlie rose from the water with an apple between his teeth, the tall teacher chose a skeleton to begin bobbing. Off went the skeleton's mask—and who should it be but Frances.

Clara was stumped. She turned toward a short ghost to her left. "Say, ghost," she whispered out the corner of her mouth, "what kid in the class dressed up as that other witch?"

The ghost shrugged its sheet-covered shoulders. "Beats me," it said through its jagged hole of a mouth. "But that other witch sure gives me the creeps."

"Ooooooooooo," said Clara, feeling more miserable than ever. "Who could that other witch be?"

All this while the witch across the circle appeared to be having a delightful time at the Halloween party. When she caught Clara's stare, a black smile sliced across her green face. She waved a bony hand merrily at Clara.

"How rude can you get? What a showoff!" Clara huffed. "So rub it in, why don't you? My costume took me all last night to make. I'll bet you anything that other witch's costume is store-bought."

The apple bobbing continued. As each mask came off Clara examined the face before it dunked into the water after an apple. One by one she checked off names in her head to determine who that other witch was.

When every girl was checked of her mental list, she asked herself, "Could that other witch be a boy? Of course. A boy could dress up as a witch, couldn't he? Just to spite me. I bet it's Roger. Only Roger would do something as creepy as copying my witch idea."

But no sooner had this crossed her mind than the tall teacher called out Roger's name, and the blue-bearded pirate stepped forward.

"It's about time," Roger said, removing his beard and kneeling beside the tub of water. "I mean, what took you so long to call on me?"

"Oooooooooooo," said Clara. "Who could that other witch be?"

Clara's next thought was this: Could there be a party crasher in our classroom—some kid from another class whose own Halloween party wasn't so hot, so she came to this one?

She counted all the students.

"One two, three, four, five . . . twenty-four, twenty-five plus me makes twenty-six," she ran off. "Say, something is fishy here. There are twenty-five kids in my class. So how come I counted twenty-six? There's an extra kid at this party. We have a party crasher and I bet the teacher doesn't even know it." And she eyed the other witch more severely.

At this point the tall teacher announced, "OK, people. Shall we take our seats? Time to eat our Halloween treats."

This was the moment Clara had been waiting for. As soon as the class broke from the circle, she marched up to the other witch. Crooked nose to crooked nose the two witches stood.

"You're in big trouble, you!" Clara snapped. "You don't belong in this room, do you? Who are you? I was meant to be the ugliest kid in the class, and I was until you came. So go back to

your own classroom, why don't you?"

The other witch's narrow black lips spread wide. Clara took a step backward. My, how toothless this other witch's mouth really appeared. Her snarled hair looked genuine as well. And her wrinkles—how did she ever get them on her face like that? Her five warts looked nothing like clay.

"Frightening party, isn't it, Missy," the other witch cackled in a voice that sent ripples through Clara's skin.

"Say, just who are you?" Clara said, in a near whisper.

"What's that, Missy?" asked the other witch. "Speak up. Speak up."

"Who are you? Where did you come from?"

The other witch raised a crooked finger that looked like an

authentic crooked finger and pointed straight up. "From four thousand feet altitude, Missy. Is that what you mean?" she answered. "Good flying height tonight, for your information— dark and stormy."

Clara folded her arms across the front of her black dress. "OK. Knock it off," she said. "Why are you really here?"

"Why, I spotted some of my friends down here having a party," replied the other witch. "So I thought I would drop down and join in the fun. Great crowd."

"You're just here to show me up, aren't you," said Clara. "I was the ugliest kid in the class before you came."

"Well, Missy, I've learned something in my two thousand years of flying," said the other witch. "That often when you think you are better than everyone else, someone will come along and prove you wrong. But now I must be off to work, Missy. Busy night for us witches, isn't it?"

And with that, the other witch turned on her high heels and stepped out the classroom door.

Clara bolted for the window. Outside on the playground a stiff wind churned up dust devils. The lone oak tree shook off its last leaves and sent them swirling around the jungle gym.

The other witch appeared on the baseball field with a broom in her hand. A black cat brushed against her leg. Near the pitcher's mound, she straddled the broom handle; her cat sat behind her. Then, with Clara watching  intently, the broom rose into the air and rocketed away.

Clara spun around. She pointed out the window and shrieked to her class, "Witch! Witch! Look, everyone! A witch! A witch!"

Only a couple of her classmates looked toward the window. Most continued to munch their Halloween cupcakes.

"Sure, Clara," Howard called out. "We know how ugly you think you are."

"You were uglier without the costume," said Roger.

"Yeah," said Frances. "You always think you're the best at everything."

"Brag, brag, brag!" said Emily.

The tall teacher, for his part, eyed Clara meaningfully and pointed to her desk in the second row.

"Well, how do you like that?" said Clara, fixing her crooked nose more firmly on her face.

And even though she was now truly the ugliest kid in the class, she said nothing more about her costume. She stepped to her desk and grabbed the cupcake off her desktop.

She wolfed it down in one bite.

The Purple Reader

Reading was difficult for Kenneth. Ever since first grade, teachers had tried to teach him the sound each letter made. And they tried to teach him how to put these sounds together to form words and how to put the words together to form sentences. But there were too many sounds for Kenneth to remember, and the words were too long for him to figure out, and the sentences were impossible to understand at all.

"Reading is screwy," Kenneth often said. "What good is reading a book, anyway, when you can watch the same story on TV or rent the movie on video? What's the point?"

As a result Kenneth was the poorest reader in the room at the end of the hall. His reading level was so low he didn't fit into either of the two reading groups. Instead, he spent each reading period sitting alone in the reading corner until the tall teacher had time to read with him in an Easy-to-Read book.

"You have the ability to be a good reader," the tall teacher often said to Kenneth. "But you must put in more effort in trying to improve."

Still Kenneth spent many lonely hours sitting there on the reading-corner rug, day after day, week after week.

One morning the tall teacher leaned against his desk, looking over his class. Many students were sprawled out on the floor reading this week's Weekly Reader. Some stood by the classroom's encyclopedias, examining the pictures of the human body. Others had just returned from the library with books tucked under their arms and sat down to read about lions and space and whales and dinosaurs.

"OK, people," said the teacher. "Please put away your books. It's time for reading."

Kenneth looked up from his desk. He raked

his fingers through his shock of red hair and wiped his nose with the side of his hand.

"Will the Red Reading Group join me at the reading table?" said the tall teacher. "The Blue Reading Group should complete the next two pages in their workbooks. And Kenneth . . ."

"I know, I know," said Kenneth, before the teacher had finished his sentence. "I'll go read by myself in the reading corner." And he rose from his desk, trudged to the back of the room and plopped down on the reading-corner rug.

The reading corner lay under the windows. The windows looked out over the playground. The rug was thick and comfortable, and there were two large stuffed pillows to prop up your head if you wanted to lie down. Books filled

three long shelves. Most were paperback chapter books, far too difficult for Kenneth to read, and the few picture books on the bottom shelf he had flipped through dozens of times already.

"It's the same boring picture books day after day," he said, scanning the bottom shelf. "I can recite every book on this shelf by heart."

He opened a book about magic tricks and tossed it aside. He spent the next five minutes staring out the window at kindergartners having recess. He pulled his arms inside his T-shirt and pretended he was a seal. He spent the following four minutes unlacing his shoes and relacing them a different way. For the next seven minutes he blew saliva bubbles on the tip of his tongue. He checked the clock. Reading period was only half over.

"Will the Blue Reading Group come to the reading table?" announced the tall teacher. "The Red Reading Group should complete the next two pages in their workbooks."

Kenneth looked toward the reading table. The tall teacher sat at one end with five students on each side of him. Howard was reading aloud from the third-grade reader.

"I wonder if I'll ever be allowed out of this reading corner to join a reading group," Kenneth said to himself. "Fat chance. If I can't read by this time, I'll never learn to do it." And he lay on his back staring at a spider swinging from the fluorescent lights.

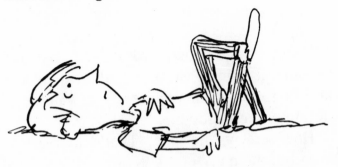

A minute later, Kenneth again scanned the bottom shelf. "Now where did I put *The Book of World Records*?" he said to himself. "I wonder if there is a record for the longest time spent in the reading corner."

As he searched the shelf his eyes fell on the spine of a book he had never seen before.

"How screwy," he said. "I thought I knew every book on this shelf."

The book had a purple leather cover and was as thick as a dictionary. Ordinarily Kenneth would have ignored a fat book like this one, but the big golden letters engraved on the book's spine caught his interest. They read:

KENNETH'S PURPLE READER

"This is screwy," said Kenneth. "How did my name get on this book?"

With one finger Kenneth pulled the purple book off the shelf. It fell onto the shag rug with a thud. He grabbed the cover and flipped the book open.

The first page delighted him—one big picture without a single word to read. Leaning forward, he saw that the picture was a watercolor painting of a classroom.

"How screwy," he said. "That's the room at the end of the hall."

Leaning farther still, he spotted a boy in the picture, sitting alone in the back corner. The boy had red hair and wore a white T-shirt.

Kenneth snatched the book in both hands. "That's me!" he said, holding the book close to his eyes. "How did I ever get into a picture book?"

Quickly Kenneth turned the page. Page two revealed another large watercolor painting. This one showed a snow-covered playground. Under the picture were three lines of writing.

"Why, it's the playground at W. T. Melon Elementary," Kenneth said, putting his nose practically on the page. "Screwier and screwier."

Studying the picture some more, he made out a lone boy standing by the slide. Again the boy looked remarkably like himself, although he wore an orange down parka much too large for him.

Kenneth's attention turned to the four lines of writing at the bottom of the page. The first word was easy enough to read—**Kenneth**.

He squinted at the next word. He always squinted while trying to figure out a new word.

"A . . . rrrrr . . . i . . . ved—Arrived, that's the word," he said. "**Kenneth arrived . . . Kenneth arrived at school.**"

Here he lowered the book and took a deep breath as if exhausted by all the reading he had

done. He raised it again and tackled the next sentences.

Snow covered the playground. Kenneth was mad because he had to wear an ugly coat to school.

Kenneth set down the purple reader and rose to his knees. He looked out the window at the playground. Except for some brown leaves blowing across it, the asphalt was bare.

"What's this book talking about?" he said. "Not a flake of snow has fallen on the playground all year. And that boy in the picture couldn't be me. I'd never be caught dead wearing an ugly orange parka to school!"

Again Kenneth turned the page, but page three was blank. *Flip! Flip! Flip!* The rest of the book was blank as well.

"Screwier and screwier," he said, snapping the book shut. "Time to take a nap until the teacher calls on me."

Kenneth forgot about the purple reader for the rest of the day. That night it snowed a foot and a half. When Kenneth walked down to breakfast he found an orange parka hanging on the back of his chair.

"I'm sorry, Kenneth, but your winter coat is still in the attic," his mother said. "It is very cold outside, so you will have to wear your father's down parka to school. I know it's a little large on you, but it will have to do for today."

As you might expect, Kenneth threw a major temper tantrum, but when the school bus pulled up in front of his house he had no choice but to grab the old orange coat and race outside.

The bus rolled up in front of W. T. Melon Elementary School. The second the door folded open, Kenneth bounded down the stairs. Overnight a thick quilt of snow had covered the playground. Icicles hung from the school's gutters like fangs. A layer of white sheathed the jungle gym, swings, and merry-go-round, and each tetherball pole wore a white top hat.

Being the first one off the bus, Kenneth got to make the first tracks across the snow-covered asphalt.

"I look like a giant pumpkin in this parka," he grumbled, stopping by the slide. That's when the picture in the purple reader dawned on him.

Three snowballs whizzed past his head as he thought, "How screwy. It happened exactly the way the purple book said it would. The book said it would snow and it said I would wear this orange coat to school. And look, here's the snow and here's the stupid coat."

The morning bell interrupted Kenneth's thoughts, and he charged toward the school door.

Tramp! Tramp! Tramp! went the sound of rubber boots as bundles of wool and nylon marched into the room at the end of the hall. Marbles of snow clung to coats, mittens, and stocking hats.

"Please deposit all icicle spears and snowballs into the sink," ordered the tall teacher.

Tramp! Tramp! Tramp! Each bundle entered the coat closet and exited as out as a rosy-cheeked, red-nosed third-grader.

For the first time in his life Kenneth was anxious for reading to begin.

"I will meet with the Red Reading Group first," announced the tall teacher. "The Blue Reading Group should do the next two pages in their workbooks. And Kenneth . . ." But Kenneth had already dived into the reading corner.

Now where was that thick purple reader? He found it on the bottom shelf and yanked it out. Lying on his belly, he reexamined the snow picture on the second page, then flipped to page three. To his surprise, he discovered a picture on it today—a watercolor of a snowman. He stood on the playground peering into the room at the end of the hall.

"What a strange-looking snowman," Kenneth told himself.

Under the picture appeared six lines of writing, slightly smaller than the ones on page two. Squinting at the words, Kenneth began to read:

A snowman stood outside the classroom window. The snowman had the usual round head and large round belly. A pair of glasses circled two rocks used for eyes, and an apple served for a mouth. But how odd! A black beard dangled from his chin. The snowman watched Kenneth read.

"Screwy," said Kenneth, shaking his head. "There's no snowman outside the window." Here he paused. He set down the book and looked up. "Is there? Could there be?"

Slowly Kenneth rose to his knees. There he was, all right, the snowman, exactly as he appeared in the purple reader picture.

Kenneth smacked his mat of red hair and

dropped onto his bottom. He grabbed the book and stared at the picture again.

"This book knows things," he said. "It told me about the snow and it told me about the snowman. Could it tell me what will happen next?"

Kenneth gulped air. With one shaky finger he turned the page.

Page four held a smaller picture with ten lines of writing beneath it. The picture showed the room at the end of the hall empty and with the lights off.

Kenneth squinted at the words. Although some were long, he was determined to read every one of them. The last lines said:

The lights suddenly went out in the classroom at the end of the hall. The teacher announced that the class could go outside and have a snowball fight . . .

"Impossible," said Kenneth. "That could never happen."

But as Kenneth spoke, the room went dark.

"Well, people, I see our school has lost electricity," the tall teacher called from the reading table. "But that snow looks inviting out the window. Let's go outside for the first snowball fight of the year."

Kenneth dropped the book he was holding. "It's true," he said. "It's screwy but true. This book can tell me the future!"

From that day on, reading period was Kenneth's favorite time of the day. Each morning when the tall teacher announced reading, Kenneth dove head-first toward the reading corner and pulled out the purple reader. Each day he discovered a new watercolor with sentences under it. Each day the pictures grew smaller and smaller and the words more plentiful, but Kenneth never failed to read every one of them.

A week after discovering the book, Kenneth turned to a picture of Emily. Recently Emily had been freed of the braces on her teeth and now wore a retainer. Kenneth read that Emily would soon reach into the lunchroom garbage can and pick up the silver wiry object.

That afternoon Emily was in tears. "I lost my new retainer!" she said to the tall teacher. "My mom will kill me if I don't find it."

Kenneth's hand shot into the air. "Emily, I bet you took your retainer out during lunch," he said. "I think you threw it away with your lunch scraps."

At once Emily raced to the lunchroom and retrieved her retainer.

"I never imagined reading could be this

interesting," Kenneth told himself.

On page ten of the purple reader Kenneth read that the fire alarm would go off at eleven-twenty, so he left his warm coat and boots on after the eleven o'clock recess. Sure enough, he was the only warm third-grader during the fire drill.

On page eleven he read that Frances would throw up in the afternoon.

"You better go to the nurse's room right now," he told Frances after lunch. "You might be embarrassed if you don't."

Frances looked at him with a green face and nodded.

"I never imagined reading could be so useful," said Kenneth, watching Frances leave the room.

After three weeks the watercolors disappeared from the purple reader. From then on when Kenneth turned to the next page he found only writing. Still, each reading period Kenneth would sit cross-legged on the reading-corner rug and decipher every word on the page.

Finally the day came when he pulled the purple reader off the bottom shelf and flipped to the final page.

"I've read this entire book," he said to himself. "I wonder what the last page could tell me."

Kenneth placed the book on his lap. Although the page contained twenty-five lines of writing and dozens of tricky-to-read words, he squinted at the page and began to read.

A big change came for Kenneth. He was no longer in the reading corner . . .

Here Kenneth hesitated. A sense of dread past through him. "A big change?" he said. "What big change? Something bad, maybe. Why aren't I in the picture? Where am I? What happened to me?"

For the first time Kenneth thought that

knowing the future might not be so exciting. He smacked his mop of red hair and lowered the book. "I can't read any more," he said. "Something bad is going to happen to me. I'm such a crummy reader maybe they'll send me back a grade. Or maybe they'll put me in that retard class for bad readers. Or even worse. Maybe I will suddenly get sick? Maybe I'll have a serious accident?"

At that moment the tall teacher stood up from the reading table. "OK, people," he said. "Will the Red Reading Group do the next two pages in their workbooks?"

"This is it," Kenneth said under his breath. "Here goes. Whatever is going to happen will happen now."

"Will the Blue Reading Group come up to the reading table?" said the tall teacher. "And Kenneth . . ."

Kenneth couldn't breathe. His heart thumped hard under his T-shirt. "What?" he called out meekly. "It's OK. I'll stay here in the reading corner. No problem. I don't mind. I'm perfectly happy here. I'll just sit here quietly and reread one of these picture books."

"Kenneth," said the tall teacher, "in the past two months your reading has improved a great deal. I've been watching you. You've been making a big effort back in the reading corner.

I always knew you had the ability. Why don't you put down that purple book and join the Blue Reading Group from now on? I don't think you will have any trouble."

Mary's Little Lamb

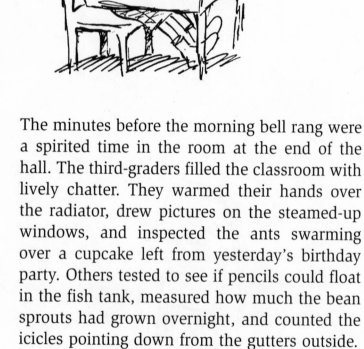

The minutes before the morning bell rang were a spirited time in the room at the end of the hall. The third-graders filled the classroom with lively chatter. They warmed their hands over the radiator, drew pictures on the steamed-up windows, and inspected the ants swarming over a cupcake left from yesterday's birthday party. Others tested to see if pencils could float in the fish tank, measured how much the bean sprouts had grown overnight, and counted the icicles pointing down from the gutters outside.

Meanwhile, in the third row by the window sat Mary. With her eyes were fixed on her desk-top, she appeared to be doing nothing. Her jaw bobbed up and down as she gnawed on a double wad of chewing gum. Every few seconds she slid an inch farther down in her seat.

Kenneth looked up from the reading corner. "There she goes again," he said. "I wonder what Mary is daydreaming about today."

"She's gone for good this time," said Clara, combing her hair by the sink. "If the fire alarm went off right now, I doubt she would even hear it."

In the front of the room, the tall teacher leaned against his desk with his eyes closed. When the morning bell rang, his eyes opened.

"OK, people," he said, punching a yawn with his fist. "Let's sit down, settle down, and quiet down. Please take out your homework. I will come around and collect your papers."

Desks opened and a sheet of paper appeared on every desktop. Every desktop but one—Mary's. Mary continued to stare at the wooden surface in front of her while sliding farther and farther down in her seat. By the time the tall teacher reached her desk, Mary was on the edge of her chair.

"Mary?" he said. "Mary, where is your homework?"

Mary remained motionless.

The teacher waved a hand in front of her face. "Mary?" he repeated, clicking his fingers.

Mary blinked and champed hard on her gum. "Here," she called out.

"Mary, you've been daydreaming again," said the tall teacher.

"I guess I was," she said, pushing herself upward.

"And Mary, you know it is against the rules to chew gum in class," said the teacher.

Mary removed her gum. "I guess I do," she said, sticking the wad on the bottom of her desk.

"And Mary, do you have your homework?"

Mary shrugged. "I guess I didn't hear the homework assignment," she said.

The tall teacher's grip tightened on the papers in his hand. The tips of his ears turned crimson. "Mary," he said, "you must start paying more attention in class. You frequently miss assignments or instructions. You are constantly forgetting things. When are you going to stop daydreaming?"

Meanwhile, Mary had slipped down in her seat again and was staring out the window.

"Mary!" the tall teacher called out.

"Here," piped Mary.

"Something must be done about your daydreaming."

Aren't daydreams peculiar things? Who knows where they come from. Those mental pictures, songs, and ideas seem to be stored in a secret closet in our heads and pop out without warning. But we need daydreams, also. How else could we make it through a long car ride or a boring afternoon at school? When else can we see whatever pictures we want to see and change them as we please?

In Mary's case, however, daydreams seemed to pop in her head more frequently and at the worst moments. She tried her best to pay attention to lessons at school, but her own imagined thoughts and pictures were more interesting and refused to go away.

"OK, people, open your reading books to page ninety-three," the tall teacher instructed. "Let's read some poems."

While the rest of the class took out their readers, Mary removed the gum from her desk bottom and stuck it in her mouth. She started staring at her thumb and slid slowly down in her chair.

At that moment the classroom door opened a crack. Everyone besides Mary saw what entered the room. Everyone besides Mary heard *click, click, click* on the tile floor.

"Ahhh!" said everyone but Mary.

Mary continued to contemplate her thumb. Not until something close by went "Baaah!" did she jolt.

She looked around and saw nothing.

"Baaah!" came the sound again, this time from under her desk. She looked at her feet and saw a little lamb. Its fleece was as white as the snow on the playground. Its pointed ears flicked, and its three-inch tail swished back and forth like a paintbrush. With big black eyes it looked pleadingly up at Mary.

"It's you again," Mary said.

"Baaah!" said the lamb.

"Ahhh!" went the class.

The tall teacher rose from his desk. Slowly he stepped to the desk in the third row by the window. He bent over and said, "Mary, what is that little lamb doing in this classroom?"

Mary shrugged. "I don't know," she said. "I spotted it this morning by my house. I guess it fol-lowed me to school today."

"To school today?"

"To school today," said Mary.

"So it followed you to school today, Mary. But that is against the rules," said the tall teacher.

"What am I supposed to do?" said Mary. "I was just walking along the sidewalk and that lamb started following me. It sat on the playground when I came inside."

"You should do what other children do when their pets come to school with them," said the tall teacher. "Take that animal outside and leave it beyond the school fence."

Mary sighed. "I guess so," she said, and trudged to the coat closet to get her coat.

Click, click, click went the little lamb's hooves on the tile floor as it tripped along behind her. *Swish, swish, swish* went its three-inch tail as it followed Mary to the door.

"And please hurry back, Mary," called the tall teacher. "You've already wasted enough class time."

"In two shakes," said Mary, stomping out the door.

By the time Mary returned, the class had finished reading poetry and was now writing cursive L's. Mary took out her pencil and wrote a perfect L, careful to stay between the lines, slanting the proper amount. But in the middle of her second L a sparkle from an icicle outside the window caught her attention. Farther and farther she slid down in her seat as a mental movie filled with jewels and glittering treasure played in her head.

At that moment the classroom door opened again.

"Aaaah," said the class as the little lamb stepped nimbly down the aisle toward Mary's desk.

"Baaah!" went the little lamb, sitting by Mary's feet.

Mary slid off her chair, nearly landing on the floor. As she pulled herself up, she looked at the fleecy creature under her desk.

"Shoo! Go away! You're embarrassing me!" she said.

The tall teacher looked up from his desk. "Mary," he said, "will you please remove that lamb from this classroom."

Mary trudged to the coat closet a second time.

"This little lamb is getting on my nerves," she said, and strode out the door with the lamb at her heels.

The lamb reappeared often that morning. Everywhere that Mary went, the lamb was sure to go. It followed her into the library and startled her as she daydreamed near the encyclopedias. It followed her into the lunchroom, and while Mary sat deep in thought, with a peanut butter and jelly sandwich halfway into her mouth, the lamb let out a bleat that almost made her gag.

Even when Mary visited the Girls' Room, the little lamb visited her. While washing her hands she stared blankly into the mirror.

"Baaah! Baaah!" went the lamb, and Mary jumped an inch.

"Enough is enough!" she screamed. "How am I ever going to get rid of you?"

That afternoon the tall teacher did a science experiment by dipping a celery stalk into a jar of red water. Already Mary's mind had drifted off. Being an expert daydreamer, she could daydream in marvelous colors and was now imagining how her classroom would look all blue, then all yellow, then all green.

"Baaah! Baaah!" went the little lamb at her feet.

"Here!" Mary jolted to attention and banged her knees on the bottom of her desk.

The tall teacher glared at the girl in the third row. His red ears told the story.

"Mary," he said through his teeth, "I told you farm animals are not allowed in this classroom. This one seems to be showing up every hour. Now it is recess time. Will you take that creature outside again and make sure it does not return?"

Head bowed, hands stuffed in her pockets, Mary traipsed out to the playground. She headed to the baseball field, now resting under a foot of snow. "Scram! Get lost!" she shouted to the little lamb, almost invisible against the white snow behind her.

"Baaah!" went the lamb. It bounded from one of Mary's footprints to the next.

Up and down, up and down Mary tramped, stamping out a giant cursive M in the snow.

"How am I ever going to get rid of you, little lamb?" she said.

"Baaah! Baaah!" cried the lamb.

Next Mary stomped out an enormous A. "What a nuisance you are, little lamb," she said.

"Baaah!" went the lamb, shaking snow off its back.

"Why are you following me, little lamb?" said Mary, flattening a giant R.

The lamb leaped into the next footprint.

"Baaah! Baaah!" it bleated.

Mary finished her name with a colossal Y. "And why do you keep interrupting my day-dreams?" she said.

At the bottom of the Y Mary stooped to pack a snowball. "You infuriate me, little lamb," she said. "I never know when you will show up. You keep startling me. I'm a nervous wreck. I haven't had a peaceful moment all day." And she smacked the snowball against the outfield fence.

When she got back to the classroom the tall teacher held up some writing paper. "Now, people, I want you to write a poem," he said.

"It should be a rhyming poem, four lines long. Be creative. You have twenty minutes to finish."

While the teacher passed out the paper, Mary turned toward the classroom door. Good. No lamb. She leaned over her paper and gripped her pencil tightly. She checked the door again before beginning to write. In one nonstop burst of energy she scribbled a line of poetry about the one thing on her mind—the little lamb.

Again she checked the door.

"That mutton has sure made me mad," she said, writing the second line. "I just know it's hanging around the school grounds, waiting to take me by surprise."

She wrote the third line and again turned toward the door.

"Still no lamb," she muttered to herself. "But I must stay alert. I'm not going to let it startle me again."

Mary composed the fourth line of her poem and made it rhyme with the second. The final period was hardly in place, however, when a paper clip on the floor caught her attention.

Mary stared at the paper clip. She had started to drop in her seat when "Baaah! Baaah! Baaah!"—louder than ever—nearly flipped her out of her chair. At her feet sat the little lamb, ears twitching and three-inch tail swishing merrily.

Mary closed her eyes and said an oath. "That did it!" she shouted. "I'm going to take you some place, little lamb, where you can never startle me again!"

Without waiting for a word from the teacher, she raced to the coat closet and put on her coat. In one swift move, she spun around, scooped up the little lamb, and tucked it under her arm.

"Baaah! Baaah!" went the lamb as Mary stomped out the door.

What happened to Mary's lamb after that, no one in the room at the end of the hall knows for sure. But the next day everyone noticed a change in Mary. Whenever she started to slip down in her seat she suddenly flinched and slid upward. Over and over her head turned toward the door. She was alert. She was constantly on her guard.

"Mary, I see you are paying much better attention today," said the tall teacher. "And I'm glad we have no more problem with your little lamb."

The tall teacher had pinned yesterday's assignment—the four-line poems—to the bulletin board. Of course, few students ever stop to read what's on a bulletin board; it's more important to peel right past it and be the first one out the door at recess time. But if the third-

graders in the room at the end of the hall had stopped to read Mary's poem, they might have found it interesting.

This is what it said:

I know this pesky little lamb.
Its wool is snowy white.
And if it follows me to school one more time,
I'll have lamb chops for dinner tonight.

The Bug in
Her Ear

"OK, OK, let's see. Number six," Rosalie read off the test paper in front of her. "What is the longest river in the United States?"

At once Rosalie turned her head toward Aaron's desk. She craned her neck to catch a glimpse of his answer sheet. She spotted number six but could read only the word Miss after it. Aaron's hand covered the rest of the answer.

Rosalie quickly copied this onto her paper. "Miss?" she said to herself. "Miss who?"

Her head swiveled toward Clara's desk. This

was better. The answer to number six was in plain view on Clara's sheet, and Clara was never wrong. The longest river in the United States was the Mississippi River. Rosalie quickly jotted it down.

Rosalie swiped her brown bangs out of her eyes with a brush of her hand. "This social studies test is certainly a lot more work than I thought it would be," she said, reading the next question. "OK, OK. What is the capital of the United States?"

Again she looked toward Aaron's desk. Drat! This time Aaron's hand covered his entire answer. Rosalie's gaze returned to Clara's paper. Drat again! Her answer was out of view as well.

Rosalie shook her head and batted her bangs again. "So now what am I supposed to?" she said under her breath.

Charlie sat in front of Rosalie. Just as she was leaning forward to peer over Charlie's shoulder, she heard something peculiar—a small voice coming from someplace very near.

"No, no, no, Miss!" it said. "You don't need to copy that answer."

Rosalie fell back in her seat. She swiveled her head from side to side. "Says who?" she said. "Who said that?"

"The capital of the United States is

Washington, D.C.," said the mysterious voice. "That stands for the District of Columbia."

Rosalie moved her eyes up and down. "OK, come on, whoever you are," she said. "That sounds like a silly name for a capital."

Rosalie spun around in her chair. Her ponytail whipped from side to side. Was Roger whispering the answer to her? Impossible. Roger knew less about social studies than she did. So who was saying those things?

Rosalie looked toward the ceiling and under her desk. "OK, OK, now," she said softly, almost to herself. "Where are you? Who are you? What are you?"

"I'm here, Miss. I'm near," came the voice again, extremely close to her right side. "I'm the tiny doodle bug in your ear."

Rosalie made a sour face. "A bug? In my ear? Oh, ick!"

From the front of the classroom

came the tall teacher's *shhhhhhhhhh.*

Rosalie looked down at her paper, pretending to work.

The bug in her ear sounded indignant. "Ick, indeed, Miss," it said. "I'll have you know I'm a bug of distinction—well-groomed and refined. And, may I add, I'm exceedingly cleaner than this ear hole in which I am sitting."

"My mother warned me something like this might happen if I didn't keep those things clean," Rosalie muttered.

"Great crop of potatoes growing in here, though," the bug put in.

Rosalie swatted her brown bangs. "OK, OK, little bug," she said uneasily. "Now that you are in my ear, what do you intend to do in there? I have this quiz to finish, you know."

"Well, Miss, don't think I'm here just to bug you or beat the drum," said the bug. "I'm here to help. And from the way I've watched you copy all your answers, I figure you can use all the help you can get."

Rosalie scowled. Regarding her test again

she said, "OK, little doodle bug, if you think you're so smart, what's the answer to number eight? How many states are there in the United States?"

"Fifty," came the immediate answer.

"Fifty!" Rosalie exclaimed a tad too loudly, so that the tall teacher looked up from his desk and gave her his famous "warning" stare.

"Are you sure fifty is the right answer, little bug?" said Rosalie, dropping her voice. "That sounds like an awful lot of states to me."

"Rely on me, Miss," said the bug. "We Bugs-in-the-Ear know the answers to everything. Just name it—math, spelling, reading, writing—I can tell you anything you need to know."

Rosalie twirled her bangs with her pointer finger. "You don't say," she said thoughtfully.

"Here's the bargain," said the bug. "Let me stay in your ear during school hours, and I'll guarantee you will never miss another fill-in-the-blank, true-or-false, or multiple-choice question on a test for the rest of your days at school."

"You mean I'll never have to copy off another paper?" said Rosalie. "Copying answers is becoming more and more difficult all the time."

"That's right, Miss. No more copying. From now on you'll just have to listen to the Bug-in-Your-Ear."

Rosalie picked up her pencil. "OK, OK, little doodle bug," she said. "It's a deal. Let's get to work."

That afternoon Rosalie's classmates received the first hint that things had changed for Rosalie. Not once during spelling did they hear the tall teacher call out, "Keep your eyes on your own paper, Rosalie," or "Rosalie, do your own work," or "You'll never learn anything by copying answers, Rosalie."

When the bell rang to go home, Rosalie felt a tickle on her cheek. Soon she spotted a tiny speck, the size of a period, skitter across her desktop. She followed the dot until it disappeared into the heart-shaped pencil sharpener she kept on the right-hand corner of her desk.

Rosalie leaned forward and whispered, "So long, little doodle bug. Nice having you in my ear. Now remember, tomorrow at eight-thirty sharp, I expect you back there helping me with answers on my math. A deal is a deal."

The next morning, with ears scrubbed clean, Rosalie sat at her desk. She faced a purple ditto sheet filled with three-place subtraction problems. She had already turned toward Clara's paper before hearing, "Two hundred fifty-six."

Rosalie beamed. "Good morning, little doodle bug," she said brightly. "How do you like my ears today?"

"Smells like bubble bath in here, Miss," the bug answered. "Now should we get to work on your math?"

"OK, OK. But are you a clever enough bug to do hard mathematics like this?"

"A Bug-in-the-Ear can answer anything," the bug reminded her. "Now, if you will, the answers are two hundred fifty-six, one hundred fifty-two, seven hundred thirty-three . . . Can you keep up with me, Miss?"

"Yes, yes," said Rosalie, furiously filling in answers.

So it went. All morning long the bug poured answers into Rosalie's head. Naturally, she had a perfect score on her spelling test. Her oral reading was also flawless and fluent, for the bug told her all the tough words as she came to them in her reader. Rosalie amazed her classmates by reciting two long paragraphs in the book without even looking at the pages.

In the afternoon the class had a writing assignment—What I Want to Be When I Grow Up. Rosalie's pencil never moved faster as the bug dictated every word, period, comma, and capital letter for her to write. At the end of the first sheet of writing, Rosalie threw open her desk to get out more paper.

"This is great, little bug," she said. "This is the best report I've ever written."

"Miss, don't interrupt!" snapped the bug in her ear. "Now where was I? Oh, yes . . . After my Oscar-winning performance in a movie, I would like to write a great novel, then be the first human on Mars."

"Boy, this sure beats copying," said Rosalie, writing as fast as she could.

"Glad to be appreciated, Miss," said the bug. "You can always rely on a Bug-in-the-Ear."

At the end of the day the tall teacher stood in front of the class with a solemn look on his face. He took a long gulp of coffee from his mug and said, "All right, people, remember on Monday you will be giving your oral reports on a famous American."

Rosalie remembered this all right. The idea of getting up in front of the entire class to talk about Neil Armstrong, the first man on the moon, had been bugging her for weeks. But as the tall teacher continued to talk about the speeches—how long they should be, how to use proper eye contact, and how many 3x5 note cards to use—Rosalie recalled the bug.

"OK, OK, little doodle bug," she whispered, practically to herself. "Are you any good at writing speeches?"

"A Bug-in-the-Ear is good at everything, Miss," the bug repeated.

"OK, then will you write me a speech about Neil Armstrong? Will you make it an especially good one? All the kids in the class are going to hear it."

"You can count on me, Miss," the bug

assured her. "Your talk will be first-rate. I'll slip you plenty of long sentences and three-syllable words to say. I'll add the right number of 'in my humble opinions,' and tell you when to clear your throat importantly and when to shake your fist in the air."

"Sounds good, little bug," said Rosalie. "But you can skip the fist-shaking part."

"You know, Miss, this speech will be a big deal for me as well," said the bug. "It's a true test of my ability. In fact, I shall invite all my friends and relations to this classroom to hear you speak."

"You mean there are other bugs like you around?" asked Rosalie.

"Certainly, Miss," replied the bug. "There is a bug for any student who wants one in his or her ear."

Rosalie watched the bug cross her desktop and enter the pencil sharpener. "Well, I can't imagine why any kid wouldn't want a bug like you," she said.

"Good night, little doodle bug."

Monday morning came. As the morning bell rang Rosalie sat at her desk shuffling through a stack of 3x5 cards she had filled with notes about Neil Armstrong. The tall teacher said you were expected to hold note cards during your speech, but Rosalie certainly had no intention of using hers.

She studied the heart-shaped pencil sharpener on her desk. "OK, OK, little doodle bug," she whispered. "Time to come out and climb into my ear."

It was at this point that Rosalie smelled something peculiar in the room. She took a deep sniff. Phew! It smelled sweet and perfumy.

Again she hailed the bug, but still there came no reply. "I bet that little bug is busy preparing my speech," she said, continuing to sort through her note cards.

Up front the tall teacher leaned against his desk. "Good morning, people," he said. "Let's begin the morning with the speeches you prepared about a famous American. Who wants to go first?"

When not a single hand went up, the tall teacher called on Charlie. Charlie trudged forward and began talking about the painter Norman Rockwell.

Meanwhile, Rosalie tapped nervously on her pencil sharpener. "OK, OK, little bug," she said, irritated. "I need you in my ear this instant. It's showtime!"

When Charlie finished, the tall teacher called on Mary, who came forward to talk about Helen Keller.

Almost in a panic, Rosalie lifted her pencil sharpener and shook out its contents. Pencil shavings sprinkled down on her desktop, but no bug.

"Come on, little buggy, where are you?" she said. "You can't let me down. We had a deal. I could be called on next."

Sure enough, when Mary finished, the tall teacher said, "Rosalie, will you now tell us about the astronaut Neil Armstrong?"

Rosalie swiped her bangs aside and grabbed her note cards. Her ponytail swished left and right as she plodded toward the front of the room. "I pray you're in my ear, little bug," she muttered under her breath. "I'm counting on you. I can't give this speech without you."

At this moment the classroom door opened. Into the room walked Mr. Leeks, the custodian. His finger was poised on the nozzle of a spray can, ready to blast the first thing that moved.

"Anything the matter, Mr. Leeks?" the tall teacher called out.

Like a hunter stalking its prey Mr. Leeks shuffled up a row of desks, his spray can aimed toward the classroom floor.

"The matter? The matter?" he said, scratching his sandpaper whiskers. "Something is always the matter in the room at the end of the hall. Bugs! Bugs everywhere! You should have been here before school started today. Tiny bugs covered this entire floor. But I took care of them. I blasted the room with my Bug-Off Bug Spray. You should have seen those buggies skedaddle out of here."

Bug spray? Rosalie stood as stiff as a yardstick in the front of the room. Did Mr. Leeks say bug spray? She felt hot and sticky. Bug spray?

"Does this mean the bug won't be in my ear during my speech?" Rosalie asked herself. "Does this mean I'm going to have to give this speech without his help?"

Mr. Leeks stumped up and down the rows of desks with his spray can at the ready. "Looks like my Bug-Off Bug Spray did the trick. Every one of those bugs is gone," he said, heading for the door. "Always something. Always something odd, something strange, something peculiar going on in this room at the end of the hall. What next?"

"Thank you, Mr. Leeks," said the tall teacher. "Now, Rosalie, you can start your speech."

For the next ten seconds Rosalie stood petrified, staring at her classmates. The 3x5 cards vibrated in her hands.

"That little bug let me down," she said under her breath. "I'm going to have to do it all by myself."

All at once a voice in her ear startled her. At first she failed to recognize the voice. It did not belong to the bug. It was her own voice, and it was trying to tell her something.

Rosalie's eyes fell on the first note card in her hand. She listened some more. The words came more clearly now. The inner voice was reciting the speech to her. Of course. Hadn't she spent hours that weekend writing all those notes? Maybe she could say the speech by herself. Why did she need a double-crossing doodle bug to tell her the words?

Rosalie brushed aside her bangs. She listened again, then said out loud, "OK, OK. Neil Armstrong was the first man to walk on the surface of the moon."

109

Who could have guessed that Rosalie was able to give such a fabulous speech? Certainly not Rosalie herself. But for the next three minutes she fascinated her audience with the life of Neil Armstrong. The words flowed out of her in clear, organized sentences. At one point in her talk, she became so excited she even shook her fist in the air.

Not until the afternoon did Rosalie hear the bug's voice in her ear again. She had a sheet on nouns and verbs in front of her. She had filled in half the answers already without copying off a single paper.

"A dance is a noun; to dance is a verb, Miss," said the Bug-in-Her-Ear.

Rosalie crammed her pencil into the pencil sharpener and twisted it slowly. "Sorry, little bug," she said. "I don't need you anymore."

"But we had a deal," the bug reminded her.

"I'm sure there are many other kids who would love a doodle bug in their ear," said Rosalie. "As for me, I'm never going to rely on anybody or anything but myself for answers again."

"Then it's farewell, Miss," said the bug. "Thanks for lending me an ear."

Rosalie never saw the bug leave. Not until she finished her language sheet did she even look up from her work.

Above the Classroom

It was recess time for the students in the room at the end of the hall. But in the back row Howard and Frances remained at their desks. Howard's head lay on his desktop, his right ear squished against the smooth surface. Frances's head rested on her fist; chin down, eyes closed, her head looked not unlike a marble bust in a museum.

So why were these two inside during recess with their heads on their desks? As you might have guessed, they were carrying out the famous punishment known in every elementary school across the country as putting your head down. So what crime, you may wonder, did this pair commit that deserved such a stiff sentence? Well, that morning Frances and Howard typed a message on the computer and stored it on Rosalie's floppy disk. Afterward, Rosalie, who had recently lost two front teeth, came to the computer, inserted her disk, and read the message that appeared on the screen:

HELLO, JACK-O'-LANTERN MOUTH

Two pairs of eyes in the back row watched as Rosalie jammed her finger on the delete button and spun around in her chair.

"You rats!" she hollered—which through the gap in her teeth sounded more like "You raths!"

How the tall teacher knew who the culprits were who wrote the message, Frances and Howard never figured out. But he instantly rose to his feet and glared right at them. Perhaps they had picked on Rosalie too many times before.

With ears bright red, the tall teacher condemned the guilty pair to remain inside for one entire recess, "With your heads down!" on their hard, cold desktops.

Now it was recess time, and the minute

hand on the clock above the green blackboard had jerked forward only twice since the class had charged out the door. Meanwhile, Frances fiddled with eraser crumbs on her desktop. She also memorized the nasty words whittled into the back of the seat in front of her.

Howard used up the minutes winking his eyes left, right, left, right, and discovered how the bulletin board seemed to shift up, down, up, down.

Up front, the tall teacher also had his head down on his desk. He had been in that position, without moving, since the beginning of recess.

"Hey, Frances," Howard whispered, despite the effort it took to talk with one cheek flattened.

"What is it?" the girl grumbled, having to lift her entire head off her fist to do so.

"I think the teacher dozed off," said Howard.

"Looks like it," said Frances. "He must be exhausted after the chewing-out he gave us."

Another minute dragged by. Things were getting tremendously boring when a curious sound—a slow, steady *skritch-skritch, skritch-skritch, skritch-skritch*—drifted down from the ceiling.

Frances and Howard sat up straight. Both

heads tossed back. As if counting every tiny hole in the acoustic tiles, they kept their eyes glued to the ceiling. In constant rhythm the sound continued—*skritch-skritch, skritch-skritch.*

Howard pointed upward. "Something's above our classroom," he said.

"Sounds like it," said Frances.

"Could be a burglar prowling around up there," said Howard.

"Or worse. Could be some wild animal planning to pounce upon a helpless kindergartner," said Frances.

A smile flashed across Howard's face.

Turning toward Frances, he said, "I think some-one should investigate that sound."

Frances grinned in the same manner. "I feel it's our duty to help the school."

Without another word, the pair slipped from their seats. After a reassuring glance toward the teacher's desk, they stole to the back of the class-room and opened the door of the coat closet.

Inside the dark closet, high up on the ceil-ing, was a square trap door. For years this door had been the object of curiosity for students in the room at the end of the hall. What was it for? Who ever used it? Where did it lead to? Howard and Frances were about to find out.

First, Frances climbed onto the empty coat hooks. From there she stepped up on the shelf that held the lunchboxes and tennis shoes. Now she could reach the trap door. With a push it swung open.

A chilly cloud of dust showered down on her as she gazed up into the square of black emptiness. The smell was of mold and oldness. She gripped the edge of the doorway and hoist-ed her slender body upward. After two kicks, her legs vanished into the black hole.

"How is it up there, Frances?" Howard called out.

"Come on, come on," a voice drifted down-ward.

With all his muscle, Howard hauled his portly body onto the shelf. He grabbed the doorway with

both hands and pulled. His feet pedaled air until Frances reached down and yanked him up beside her.

The pair sat side by side on the dusty floor of an immense attic. When their eyes adjusted to the dimness, they found themselves sur-rounded by a remarkable assortment of junk—pyramids of old desks, stacks of chairs, ancient globes, an abacus, a model of a giant tooth, two grinning skeletons, a flag bearing forty-eight stars, and filing cabinets teetering on top of one another like so many baby blocks.

A layer of silvery dust shrouded every object. The dust caught an occasional sparkle from a light hanging somewhere in the distance.

"Listen," Howard whispered.

Skritch-skritch, skritch-skritch.

"It's coming from the direction of the light," said Frances. "Come on." And she headed off between a stuffed raccoon and an aluminum Christmas tree with Howard close behind her.

The two explorers made their way past stacks of old books. These leather-bound encyclopedias, textbooks, and dictionaries stood in long, tall rows, arranged in such odd angles that they formed a twisting maze.

Frances and Howard walked slowly and silently. The book-stack labyrinth led them left and right, forward and backward, zigzagging into dead ends and around in circles. At last, when the light shone nearly overhead and the *skritch-skritch* sound was quite clear, the maze ended.

A final turn brought the pair into a large dusty room formed by four more book stack-walls.

"Apples," said Howard, upon examining the

room. "Everything is covered with them."

"Looks like it," said Frances.

Indeed there seemed to be an apple stitched, stenciled, or painted on every object in the place. Watercolor paintings of apples hung from the walls. Apples were carved into the legs of a wooden chair and table. The cupboards bore paintings of apples and a quilt printed with apple designs covered a dusty bed. The dusty light hanging from the ceiling wore a shade in the shape of an apple, and the pigeons fluttering in the rafters overhead occasionally dropped a white spot onto an apple-shaped rug.

Frances and Howard took this all in before their eyes fell upon a rocking chair with its back bent into the shape of an apple. *Skritch-skritch, skritch-skritch,* it went each time it rocked back and forth.

In the chair sat a large, burly man with a dusty black beard. His eyes were closed and his chin rested on a red bowtie above his broad chest. A rim of frizzy black hair circled a bald spot on his head like a bird's nest. A dusty book lay open in his large lap. The man's bearded face, his rumpled tweed jacket, and the wire-rimmed spectacles ready to drop off the end of his nose were familiar, for this was the very man whose picture hung above the

doorway of W. T. Melon Elementary School.

"It's Walter T. Melon," Howard whispered. "W. T. Melon himself."

"It looks like him," said Frances. "But I thought he was dead or something."

The man's eyes opened. He raised his head and pushed back his spectacles with a finger. Noticing the visitors he smiled through his whiskers.

"Ah, wonderful ones," he said. "What took you so long to get here?" He snapped his book shut, and a spout of dust shot upward. "Frances and Howard, come in. Come in."

Frances and Howard exchanged glances. Not until a pigeon dropping smacked the floor behind them did they step into the room.

"That's right. Come in. Take a seat," said Mr. Melon, gesturing toward a sofa. "Don't stand on politeness. Please sit down."

The two third-graders sidled across the room. They sat on the edge of a sofa uphol-stered with an apple pattern. Their eyes remained fixed on the large, dusty man slowly rocking in his chair.

Finally Howard ventured to say, "Can I ask you something?"

Mr. Melon locked his fingers together across his ample stomach. "Certainly, Howard," he said. "Questions are an excellent way to learn something about anything."

"How did you know we were coming?" asked Howard. "How did you know our names?"

"Ah, another excellent way of learning something about anything is by listening," said the man. He cupped a hand behind his ear. "And when you live above a classroom as I do, you learn many important things. Now listen."

Frances and Howard sat perfectly still. Sure enough, they could hear the tall teacher's raspy snores coming up through the floorboards.

"You see, wonderful ones," said Mr. Melon, "I hear everything that goes on in the room at the end of the hall—every question and every answer, every moan and groan, every grind of the pencil sharpener and squeak of chalk, every snicker, song, whispered secret, hiccup, cheer, and every word your teacher says, softly or shouted. Of course I overheard his ranting and raving this morning. So tell me—I've been waiting all morning to hear—what message did you leave Rosalie on the computer?"

Frances and Howard grinned together. Perhaps here was someone who could appreciate a good practical joke. As they told the story, Mr. Melon rocked in his chair and stroked his beard. When the story was over he slapped his knee once, sending up another spout of dust.

"Very creative," he said. "How did you ever come up with such a clever idea? Originality is also an excellent way to learn something about anything. Now how about a snack? Help yourselves to an apple."

Mr. Melon's guests reached for two shiny red apples in a bowl on the table. In unison they took large, juicy bites. No apple ever tasted better.

While munching, Frances studied the tall book stacks that formed the walls of the little room. She swallowed. "Looks like you do a lot of reading, Mr. Melon," she said. "Isn't reading another excellent way to learn something about anything?"

"Mr. Leeks, our custodian, told us you were

once a great teacher," added Howard.

Mr. Melon's smile doubled in length. "Once a teacher, always a teacher," he said. "Indeed, I was one of the original teachers."

"Original teachers?" said Frances.

"You mean there was a time before teachers?" asked Howard.

Here Mr. Melon rocked forward in his chair until his visitors could see twinkles in his black eyes. "Oh, no, wonderful ones," he said. "There were always teachers. But there was a time before teachers lived on this continent. And I was on the first boat that brought them here."

Frances froze with her apple near her lips. "But where were the teachers before that?" she said.

"Yeah, where do teachers come from?" Howard asked.

Mr. Melon leaned farther forward. "Apple Island," he said, lowering his voice. "An island far out in the Atlantic Ocean. Even the most clever satellites in space have yet to detect our island. A thick layer of chalk dust shrouds it most of the year."

Frances and Howard again bit into their apples at the same time. They looked at the burly man with eyes that said, "Go on, go on."

"Now, I'm sorry to tell you, for centuries

Apple Island was divided between the teachers in the north and the teachers in the south," Mr. Melon continued. "The south, you might be interested to learn, is where only crabapples grow. That's where crabby teachers come from. I lived in the north, filled with marvelous mead-

ows, splendid coffee plantations, and orchards of those delicious apples you are eating."

"But why did you leave?" asked Howard.

"Sounds like a wonderful place," said Frances.

Mr. Melon's smile disappeared. "The northern teachers and the southern teachers had a squabble," he said solemnly. "Not unlike some of the squabbles I hear down below in the room at the end of the hall. Neither side would give in. Neither side would say I'm sorry. Not even our leader, Prince Apple, who lived in the Office Palace at the foot of Chalk Mountain, could solve this dispute. So the northern teachers built an ark and left."

"And you sailed to America," said Frances.

"And built schools," said Howard

"Precisely, wonderful ones," said Mr. Melon. "And we built classrooms in the fashion of our former houses. And next to each school we built a miniature version of the Grand Playground that ran for miles across Apple Island."

Frances and Howard champed on their apples as they tried to picture a mile-long playground. A splatter of pigeon droppings woke them from their daydreams.

"But what are you doing up here?" said Frances.

"Why do you live above our classroom?" asked Howard.

"It's time to show you something," said Mr. Melon.

Here the man rose to his feet and stepped over to a dusty shelf on the back wall. He picked up a large vial filled with purple smoke. When he pulled off the stopper, Francis and Howard caught the scent of something familiar, the aroma of a classroom on a Monday morning—part Janitor floor wax, part Magic Marker, part smelly tennis shoe.

"*Voila!*" said Mr. Melon, swirling the glass container. The purple smoke spun like a tornado. "See. See what's in there."

Amidst the smoke Frances and Howard saw images of numbers and letters all whirling madly around the vial.

"What's it for?" said Frances.

"Is it dangerous?" asked Howard.

"Perfectly harmless," said Mr. Melon. "It's a mixture of chalk dust, pencil shavings, eraser crumbs, and a special ink brought with me from Apple Island."

"So what good is that purple stuff?" said Frances.

"What have you done with it?" asked Howard.

The burly man paced the room from one book wall to another, swirling his vial. "I've sprinkled this elixir in every school in the world," he said. "My formula is what makes a classroom an extra marvelous place. After all, if boys and girls are made to spend one hundred eighty days a year in them, shouldn't classrooms be the most wondrous of places?"

"I've been in classrooms since kindergarten and never found anything special about them," said Frances.

"Me neither," said Howard.

"Oh, wonderful ones," said Mr. Melon. "Has your teacher ever called on you to answer a tricky math problem and suddenly you hear the answer from somewhere in the back of the room?"

"I suppose," Frances admitted.

"And did you ever forget to do your home-work and that turns out to be the day your teacher is absent?"

"Yeah, once," said Howard.

Mr. Melon slapped the side of his pants, causing more dust clouds. "That is my Apple Island potion at work," he said. "But of course those are simple tricks. My latest formula, here in this vial, is much stronger—new and improved. In fact, this latest potion is still being tested in my laboratory."

Howard gave the room a quick once-over. "This is your laboratory?" he said, as a white pigeon dropping fell near his feet.

"Doesn't look like it," said Frances.

"But my laboratory isn't here. It's down below. My laboratory is your classroom—the room at the end of the hall. That's where my strongest elixir is tested."

Before Howard and Frances had a chance to ask what Walter T. Melon meant by this, the dusty man stopped his pacing and held a finger to his lips.

From below came the stomping of shoes and the sound of muffled voices.

"Recess is over," said Frances. "Our class is coming in."

"We have to get out of here," whispered Howard.

"How quickly recess time can pass," said Mr. Melon, returning to his rocker. "I've enjoyed our talk, wonderful ones. A good conversation is an excellent way to learn something about anything."

Like two frightened mice, Frances and Howard darted from the room and through the book maze. At the trap door they peered down into the coat closet.

Directly below them, Rosalie was hanging up her jacket. She left the closet unaware of the two pairs of legs dangling over her head. The instant the closet door closed, two bodies fell to the floor, landing in a jumbled pile of legs and arms.

Howard rose to his feet, slapping the dust off his pants. "Now we're in for it," he said.

"Looks like it," said Frances. "Just wait until the teacher catches us coming out of here."

Upon emerging from the closet, however, the pair found the class sitting quietly at their seats. Up front the tall teacher's head remained on his desk. His snores filled the classroom.

Frances and Howard smiled at each other. Without a word they raced to the computer. They found Rosalie's floppy disk and inserted it into the disk drive.

"What should we write this time?" asked Frances.

Howard pointed to the ceiling. "Do you believe all that stuff Mr. Melon told us up there?" he asked. "You know, about Apple

Island and his special elixir."

"Not a chance," said Frances. "He was just a batty old man who has been up with the pigeons too long."

As she spoke, the computer screen flashed. Frances and Howard shot back in their chairs. They gawked at the large words appearing on the screen.

THANKS FOR THE VISIT.
COME AGAIN SOON.
W. T. MELON